The Night After Christmas

by JAMES STEVENSON

 GREENWILLOW BOOKS, New York

writing from the Publisher, Greenwillow Books,
a division of William Morrow & Company, Inc.,
105 Madison Avenue, New York, N.Y. 10016.
Printed in U.S.A.   First Edition 5 4 3 2 1

Library of Congress
Cataloging in Publication Data
Stevenson, James (date)   The night after Christmas.

Summary: Tossed in garbage cans after they
are replaced by new toys at Christmas, a teddy
bear and a doll are befriended by a stray dog.

[1. Teddy bears–Fiction. 2. Dolls–Fiction.
3. Toys–Fiction] I. Title.
PZ8.9.S773Ni [E]   81-1022
ISBN 0-688-00547-0 AACR2
ISBN 0-688-00548-9 (lib. bdg.)

It was the night after Christmas. Teddy was in the garbage. "Jingle bells, Jingle bells," he sang. "Jingle all the way…"

"Why are you singing?" said a doll who was in the garbage next door.
"I don't know," said Teddy. "It's better than *not* singing."
"So you got thrown out, too?" said the doll.
"Sure did," said Teddy. "The kid who owned me got a space gun
 for Christmas."

"My name is Annie," said the doll.
"I'm Teddy," said Teddy.
"Merry Christmas, Teddy," said Annie.
"Same to you, Annie," said Teddy.

"The kid I belonged to," said Annie, "got a doll with
hair you can curl and clothes you can change plus a bikini."

"Want to sing 'Jingle Bells'?" said Teddy.
"Not right now," said Annie.

"A word to the wise," said a voice. "They collect the garbage
here first thing in the morning." It was a brown dog.

"Where can we go?" asked Annie.
"You can come to my place," said the dog.
"Thank you," said Teddy.
"Climb aboard," said the dog. "My name's Chauncey."

"It's not fancy," said Chauncey, "but it's warm."

They all went to sleep.

In the morning, Teddy said, "What do we do now?
There's nobody to play with."
"I'll play with you," said Chauncey.
"Thanks," said Teddy, "but I meant children."

"Nothing personal, Chauncey," said Annie.
"That's O.K." said Chauncey. "I'm not much for games anyway.
I run, bark, and wag my tail. That's about it."
Chauncey went out to hunt up some breakfast.

"You know what we should do?" said Teddy.

"What?" said Annie.

"We should fix ourselves up as new toys," said Teddy. "The kind kids want."

"I am what I am," said Annie. "I can't be anything else."

"Well, I can," said Teddy. "I could be on television.
 Kids love that."
"No you couldn't," said Annie.
"You'll see," said Teddy. "Clap if you like it."

Teddy climbed into a box.
"Everybody in the whole family loves Yummy!"
said Teddy. "Tell Mom to buy the large size today!
It's nourishing and delicious!"

"You didn't clap," said Teddy.
"I didn't like it that much," said Annie.
"I have a better idea," said Teddy.
 He went away for a moment.

"What are you supposed to be?" said Annie.
"I am a toy computer," said Teddy.
"Ask me a question."
"How can you be so stupid?" said Annie.
"Is that the question?" said Teddy.

"What now?" said Annie.
"Don't you know a creature from outer space
  when you see one?" asked Teddy.

    Chauncey came back.
"Having a good time?" he asked.
"No," said Teddy.
"Far from it," said Annie.
"Oh, well," said Chauncey. "You'll get used to it."

For the next few days, Teddy and Annie just sat around,
feeling sadder and sadder.

Teddy began to pace back and forth, back and forth.
"What's the problem?" asked Chauncey.
"I can't get used to getting used to it," said Teddy.

"Hmmm," said Chauncey. He started to leave.
"Where are you going?" said Annie.
"Can we come, too?" said Teddy.
"No," said Chauncey. He was gone a long time.

When Chauncey came back, he wouldn't tell them where he'd been.
"You'll find out tomorrow," he said.

The next day he took them down the street.
"Wait till you see," he said.

They stopped at a big building.
"What's so special?" asked Annie.

"You sit there, Annie," said Chauncey, "and you sit there, Teddy."
"I hear a bell ringing," said Annie.

Suddenly, children began pouring out of the doors.

They made a lot of noise, and it took a long time.

When all the children were gone,

Annie and Teddy were gone, too.

The End